CLASSIC FAIRY TALES

RAPUNZEL

Retold by James Reeves

Illustrated by Sophie Allsopp

MACDONALD YOUNG BOOKS

First published in Great Britain in 1997
by Macdonald Young Books
61 Western Road
Hove
East Sussex BN3 1JD

Designed by Shireen Nathoo Design

Typeset in 20pt Minion
Printed and bound in Belgium by Proost International Book Co.

British Library Cataloguing in Publication Data available.

ISBN: 0 7500 2031 8
ISBN: 0 7500 2032 6 (pb)

There was once a poor couple who lived in a cottage at the edge of a wood. At the back of the cottage was a little window which looked out over a high stone wall. Beyond the wall was a most beautiful garden, where grew all manner of flowers and herbs. The couple had not been inside it, for it belonged to a cruel witch named Gothel.

Now in that garden there grew a herb called rampion, which is used for making salads. In that country it was known as rapunzel.

"Ah, husband," sighed the poor woman one day, "I don't feel well, but I believe I would get better if only I had some of that rampion to eat."

So that evening, the man climbed over the wall and seized a handful of the rampion. Then he scrambled back and gave it to his wife. When she had eaten it, she felt better.

But next day it was just the same.

"Oh, I shall die," said she, "if I can't have more of that herb."

And indeed she looked so pale and ill that her husband went once more into the garden and took a bunch of the rampion. He was just going to climb back over the wall when the witch came and saw him.

"Aha!" she cried. "What are you doing in my garden?"

"Oh, madam," said the poor man, "my wife is very ill. She says that if she can't get this herb to make into a salad she will die. Please, I beg you, let me keep it."

At this the witch seemed to take pity on the man.

"Very well," she said, "you may keep it. You have no children yet, but soon your wife is to have a daughter. In payment for the rampion, you must allow me to have the child when it is born!"

What could the poor man do but agree? For he thought that otherwise his wife would die.

So every evening he went into the witch's garden for a bunch of the herb his wife so much desired. She seemed to get better every day, and at last her little girl was born.

Almost immediately the cruel witch appeared at her bedside and demanded the baby. So the poor couple were obliged to give up their only child. Gothel laughed with glee and took the baby away, to bring up as her own. She named her Rapunzel after the herb.

Every day the child grew stronger, until she could be seen playing in the witch's beautiful garden. Sometimes her parents caught a glimpse of her running amid the flowerbeds, chasing a butterfly or calling to the birds, while her golden hair waved behind her in the breeze.

But when Rapunzel was twelve years old, the cruel witch took her away from the garden and shut her in a tall, dark tower in the middle of a forest. Now this tower was built of stone and had no door and no stairs, but only a window at the top. Hour after hour Rapunzel would sit at the window looking out on the forest or singing to herself. And when the witch wanted to get to her, she would call, "Rapunzel, Rapunzel, let down your long hair." The girl's hair was so long and fine, like spun gold, that it came nearly to the ground, and was as strong as a cord. She would twist it round one of the bars of the window, and the witch would climb up it like a ladder.

So the years passed. Rapunzel grew into a fair and graceful maiden, and the witch hated her beauty and vowed she would keep her in the high tower for ever.

One day, some years later, it happened that the king's son passed by the stone tower when Rapunzel was singing to herself in her lonely room. He stopped and listened, for never had he heard so beautiful a voice.

The young prince longed to know who it was who sang with such a clear, lovely voice, and he rode up to the tower, but nowhere could he find a door. The prince could do nothing but turn his horse's head and ride home.

Next day he came again, so enchanted was he by the sound of Rapunzel's voice, and every day he came, but never could he find a way into the tall tower.

Then one day he was just approaching it when he saw the witch a little way ahead of him. He hid behind a tree to see what she did.

"Rapunzel, Rapunzel," called the witch, "let down your long hair!"

Then the prince was astonished to see a long rope of spun gold being twisted round one of the bars of the window and let down to the ground. Next, he saw Gothel climb nimbly to the window and squeeze through.

So he rode home, and next day he came again towards evening. He stood below the window and called softly, "Rapunzel, Rapunzel, let down your long hair."

He waited a moment, then the same thing happened as he had seen the day before. The long coil of gold hair fell almost to his feet; so, looking round to see that the witch was nowhere near, he climbed swiftly to the top of the tower and got in through the window.

At first Rapunzel was frightened to see the strange young man instead of the old witch. But he spoke to her in friendly tones, and she thought he was kinder and gentler than Gothel.

"Don't be afraid, sweet maiden," said the king's son. "I do not come to harm you."

So he sat down, and they talked, and the prince told Rapunzel of the world outside the tower, and of the great country over which his father the king ruled.

He came to see her every evening, until one day he said to her:

"Rapunzel, I am a prince, and I wish no one but yourself to be my princess. Will you marry me?"

Rapunzel, who loved him dearly, answered, "Yes," and put her hand in his. Then he told her that as soon as he could get her out of the stone tower, he would make her his wife.

"Every day when you come to see me," said Rapunzel, "bring me a skein of silk. Then I shall weave a ladder, and with this I shall escape out of the window and get safely to the ground."

The prince did as she said. Every evening he came to the tower and climbed up to Rapunzel and gave her a skein of silk, so that before long she had almost woven the ladder for her escape.

17

The witch Gothel knew nothing of this until one unlucky day Rapunzel said to her:

"Tell me, Gothel, how is it that when you climb up my hair, you are so much heavier than the young prince who visits me? Why, he seems to fly up in no time."

Now this was a foolish thing to say, but Rapunzel did not know how angry the witch would be.

"Oh, you wicked girl!" screamed Gothel. "So you have visitors, have you? Well, I shall put an end to your tricks, you deceitful child!"

So she took out her sharp scissors and snip-snap! in a moment she had cut off all Rapunzel's beautiful hair. Next, she spirited her from the tower and led her away to a

wild and dreary wilderness. She left Rapunzel there to wander about looking for roots and berries to keep herself from starving.

Then Gothel returned to the tower and fixed Rapunzel's long coil of hair to the bar of the window, and waited. When the prince came and called, "Rapunzel, Rapunzel, let down your long hair," she threw down the golden coil at his feet. Lightly he climbed to the window, expecting to see the sweet face of his love, Rapunzel. Instead, he saw the cruel mocking eyes of the witch, Gothel.

"So you are the prince who comes sneaking through the forest to see the little bird in the stone cage!" cried the witch in triumph. "Well, the bird has flown, my beauty, and you will never see her again!

Instead, the old cat will scratch out your eyes, you meddling thief!"

"Never!" cried the prince in anger and despair.

So saying, he leapt from the window and fell upon the ground.

But he was not killed, only bruised and shaken, for he had fallen into some thorn bushes. Alas! the thorns stuck in his eyes and, blinded, he wandered away, almost mad with grief and pain.

Rapunzel, meanwhile, struggled on through the stone desert that Gothel had banished her to. She seemed to go round and round in circles, for there was no way out. One day she tried to cheer herself by singing in a voice now small and shaking, and yet with something of its old sweetness.

The wind carried the notes of her song across the wilderness to the ears of the prince, who, almost dead from weakness and despair, had at last reached the place where Rapunzel wandered.

"What is that sound?" he cried feebly.

"Surely that is her voice – or do I imagine it?"

Blindly he stumbled towards the place where the sound seemed to be, calling out as best he could, "Rapunzel, Rapunzel, where are you?"

Then she saw him. She ran towards him, crying, "My prince, is it you? Have you found me at last?"

Then she saw that he was blind. She ran to him and put her arms about him; and the prince, so overcome with joy and faint from thirst and hunger, dropped at her feet. The girl wept to see him in such a sorry state; and as she looked down at his tired, thin face, the tears fell from her eyes on to his. Rapunzel's tears entered his eyes, and he received his sight back again. He looked up at her face and saw her almost as clearly as he had seen her when first he climbed up her golden hair to the window in the high tower.

Somehow they found their way out of the dreary wilderness, and the first thing they did was to go to the king's palace; and the king knew all about Rapunzel's mother and father, and how they had had to give up their only child to the cruel witch. So the poor man and his wife were sent for, and the prince and Rapunzel were married.

As for Gothel, they shut her up in her own high tower and kept her there. But the tower was struck by lightning in a great storm and crashed to the ground. And the witch vanished, to be seen no more.

Other titles available in the Classic Fairy Tales series:

Cinderella
Retold by Adèle Geras   Illustrated by Gwen Tourret

The Ugly Ducking
Retold by Sally Grindley   Illustrated by Bert Kitchen

Beauty and the Beast
Retold by Philippa Pearce   Illustrated by James Mayhew

Little Red Riding Hood
Retold by Sam McBratney   Illustrated by Emma Chichester Clark

Rapunzel
Retold by James Reeves   Illustrated by Sophie Allsopp

Jack and the Beanstalk
Retold by Josephine Poole   Illustrated by Paul Hess

Snow White and the Seven Dwarfs
Retold by Jenny Koralek   Illustrated by Susan Scott

Hansel and Gretel
Retold by Joyce Dunbar   Illustrated by Ian Penney

Thumbelina
Retold by Jenny Nimmo   Illustrated by Phillida Gili

Snow-White and Rose-Red
Retold by Antonia Barber   Illustrated by Gilly Marklew

Sleeping Beauty
Retold by Ann Turnbull   Illustrated by Sophy Williams

Rumpelstiltskin
Retold by Helen Cresswell   Illustrated by John Howe

Goldilocks and the Three Bears
Retold by Penelope Lively   Illustrated by Debi Gliori